# Little Critter's
# THIS IS MY SCHOOL

## BY
## MERCER MAYER

*For Gina*

A Golden Book • New York
Western Publishing Company, Inc., Racine, Wisconsin 53404

Today is my first day
of school.

I have new things
to wear.

I have a new pencil
and a notebook.

Mom gives me
money for lunch.

Mom gives me
an apple for
the teacher.

But I want
to give the teacher
my new bug.
Mom says an apple
is better.

Mom waits with me
for the school bus.

She does not have to wait,
because I am big.
But it makes her happy.

9

The bus is full.
The driver is quiet.
But we are not.
We are having fun.

I know where to go.
But I ask someone anyway.

My teacher is Miss Kitty.
I give her my apple.

We put our things away.
We have a lot of things!

Miss Kitty gives us
name tags.

I sit at my desk.
There are many kids
I do not know.

17

Everyone has to tell
something about himself.
I tell about going camping.
The bear took our food.

We learn a song.
Some kids do not sing.

FOR MISS KITTY

We draw pictures.
I draw my family.

Then we go play outside.

After playtime Miss Kitty
reads a story.

The bell rings.
It is time for lunch.
I buy lunch
all by myself.

I sit with some
other kids.
We trade food.

After lunch we have
rest time.
I am not tired.
But I have to
lie down anyway.

After rest time
we go to the library.

We have the most books
in the world.

We meet the school nurse.

Then we see a film
about dinosaurs.
I am not scared.
Dinosaurs are all
dead anyway.

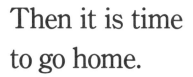

Then it is time
to go home.

Miss Kitty helps us
onto the bus.

Tomorrow is show-and-tell.
I think I will bring
my pet snake.